ANIMAL OPPOSITES
FAST AND SLOW

by Cecilia Minden

Cherry Lake Publishing • Ann Arbor, Michigan

1

Published in the United States of America
by Cherry Lake Publishing
Ann Arbor, Michigan
www.cherrylakepublishing.com

Reading Adviser: Marla Conn, ReadAbility, Inc.

Photo Credits: © Olga_i/Shutterstock Images, cover, 8; © ravipat/
Shutterstock Images, 4; © Stripped Pixel/Shutterstock Images, 6;
© OPIS Zagreb/Shutterstock Images, 10; © Volt Collection/Shutterstock
Images, 12; © worldswildlifewonders/Shutterstock Images, 14; © Beth
Swanson/Shutterstock Images, 16; © Liquid Productions, LLC/Shutterstock
Images, 18; © CreativeNature R.Zwerver/Shutterstock Images, 20; © Mark
Beckwith/Shutterstock Images, 20; © mariait/Shutterstock Images, 20;
© Vilainecrevette/Shutterstock Images, 20

Library of Congress Cataloging-in-Publication Data
Minden, Cecilia, author.
  Fast and slow / by Cecilia Minden.
     pages cm. —(Animal opposites)
  Audience: K to grade 3.
  Summary: "This Level 1 guided reader illustrates examples of "fast and
slow" found in the animal kingdom. Students will develop word recognition
and reading skills while learning about opposites and animal habits."—
Provided by publisher.
  ISBN 978-1-63470-472-4 (hardcover)—ISBN 978-1-63470-592-9 (pbk.)—
ISBN 978-1-63470-532-5 (pdf)—ISBN 978-1-63470-652-0 (ebook)
 1. Animals—Juvenile literature. 2. Speed—Juvenile literature.
3. Concepts—Juvenile literature. 4. Vocabulary. I. Title.
  QL49.M65 2016
  590—dc23
                                          2015026046

Cherry Lake Publishing would like to acknowledge
the work of the Partnership for 21st Century Skills.
Please visit www.p21.org for more information.

Printed in the United States of America
Corporate Graphics

TABLE OF CONTENTS

Pets

This rabbit lives outside. It can hop very fast.

What Do You See?

What shapes are on the tortoise's shell?

A **tortoise** is very slow. It takes its time.

Farm Animals

A horse can **gallop**. Horses like to run fast and far.

A **mule** is slow. It carries things on its back. It walks up a path.

What Do You See?

What is the pattern on the cheetah's fur?

Zoo Animals

Cheetahs are the fastest land **mammals** in the world.

A **sloth** likes to nap. Sloths are very slow.

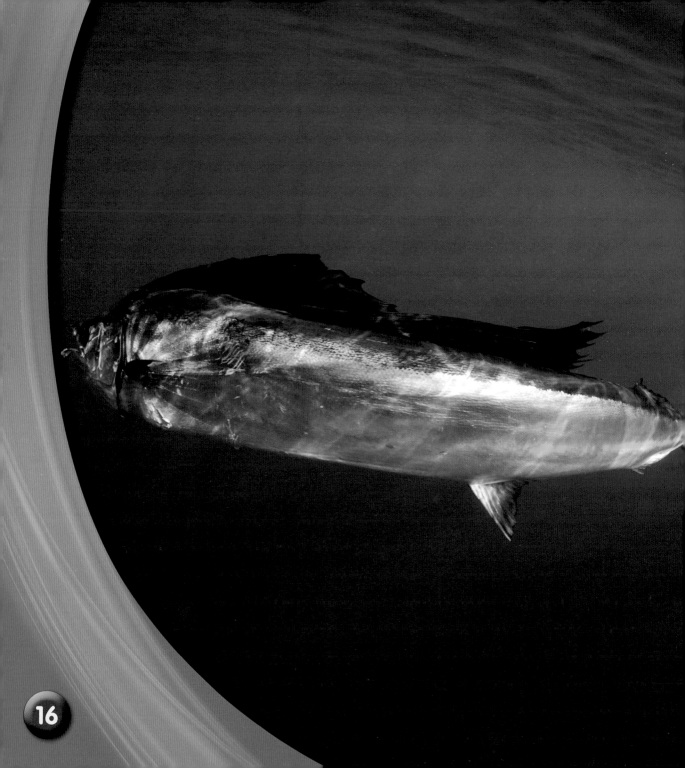

Water Animals

A **sailfish** swims fast. It uses its fins.

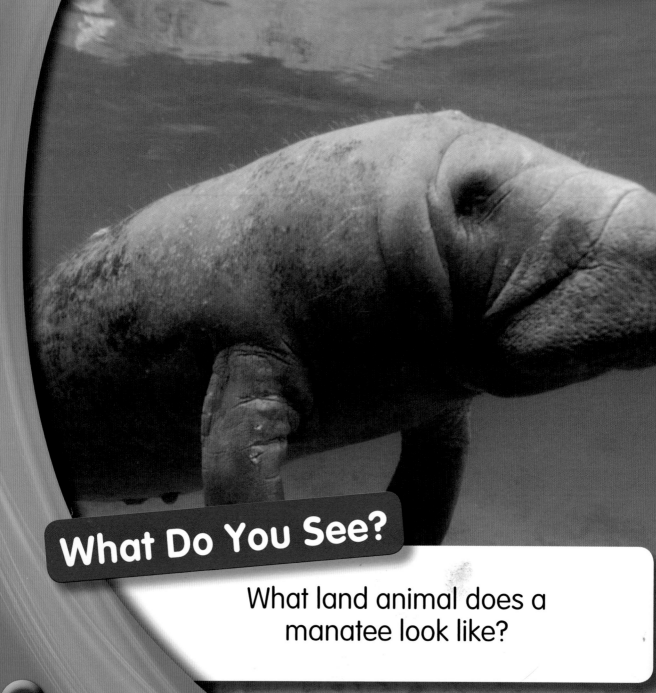

What Do You See?

What land animal does a manatee look like?

A **manatee** swims slowly.
It uses its flippers.

Which animals are fast?

Which animals are slow?

Find Out More

BOOK

Horáček, Petr. *Animal Opposites*. Somerville, MA: Candlewick
 Press, 2013.

WEB SITE

The Activity Idea Place—Opposites
www.123child.com/lessonplans/other/opposites.php
Play some games to learn even more opposites.

Glossary

gallop (GAL-uhp) to run fast using a pattern of natural
foot movements

mammals (MAM-uhlz) animals that are warm-blooded, give
birth to live babies, make milk, and breathe air

manatee (MAN-uh-tee) a large, plant-eating ocean mammal

mule (MYOOL) an animal born to a female horse and
male donkey

sailfish (SAYL-fish) a large fish that can swim fast and change
its colors

sloth (SLAWTH) a mammal with a shaggy coat that moves slowly
and lives in the trees

tortoise (TOR-tuhs) a turtle, especially one that lives on land

Home and School Connection

Use this list of words from the book to help your child become a better reader. Word games and writing activities can help beginning readers reinforce literacy skills.

animal	lives	slow
back	look	slowly
carries	mammals	swims
cheetahs	manatee	takes
farm	mule	things
fast	nap	time
fastest	outside	tortoise
fins	path	uses
flippers	pattern	very
fur	pets	walks
gallop	rabbit	water
hop	sailfish	what
horse	shapes	which
its	shell	world
land	sloth	zoo

Index

About the Author

Cecilia Minden, PhD, is a former classroom teacher and university professor. She now enjoys working as an educational consultant and writer for school and library publications. She has written more than 150 books for children. Cecilia lives in and out, up and down, and fast and slow in McKinney, Texas.